THE
FOX HUNT

THE
FOX HUNT
SVEN NORDQVIST

Morrow Junior Books
New York

Copyright © 1986 by Sven Nordqvist
First published in Sweden
under the title RÄVJAKTEN
by Bokforlaget Opal AB,
Stockholm, Sweden in 1986

Printed in the United States of America.
1 2 3 4 5 6 7 8 9 10
LIBRARY OF CONGRESS
Library of Congress Cataloging-in-Publication Data
Nordqvist, Sven.
[Rävjakten. English]
The fox hunt.
p. cm.
Translation of: Rävjakten.
Summary: Farmer Festus and his cat find a way of getting rid of a
troublesome fox by using their brains instead of a gun.
ISBN 0-688-06881-2. ISBN 0-688-06882-0 (lib. bdg.)
[1. Foxes—Fiction. 2. Cats—Fiction. 3. Farm life—Fiction.
4. Hunting—Fiction.] I. Title.
PZ7.N7756Fo   1988
[E]—dc19
87-28197
CIP
AC

THE FOX HUNT

Farmer Festus and his cat, Mercury, lived on a little farm in the country.

They had hens in the hen house, wood in the woodshed, and tools in the toolshed. They didn't get much company, and that was just fine with Festus.

But one day their neighbor Hiram dropped by. Mercury took one look at Hiram's hound and bounded right up onto Festus's hat. "Have you met up with the fox yet, Festus?" Hiram asked.

"Not that I've noticed," said Festus.

"You'd notice if he raided your hen house, all right. He stole one of my birds last night. But he won't get another chance if I can help it. Get your gun, Festus. Just because I'm locking up my hens doesn't mean he won't come calling on yours."

And Hiram and his hound stalked off.

"We'd better lock up the hens, eh Mercury?" said Festus.

"I'd say lock up Hiram," the cat hissed. "I wouldn't trust that old man with a gun."

"Don't you think he should shoot the fox to keep him from the chickens?"

"I'd never shoot a fox when I could trick him instead," Mercury replied.

"Mercury, you're right." Festus beamed at his cat. "Let's think how we can scare that fox so he'll never want to eat another hen."

So Festus puzzled and pondered all morning long. Suddenly he snapped his fingers and said, "Have you ever built a hen, Mercury?"

"I certainly have not ever built a hen," the cat replied.

"Well then, let's go build one," said Festus. "You'd better stick by me so the fox doesn't get you."

"Just let him try," Mercury said, and he followed Festus to the toolshed.

Festus hunted up a white balloon and a dozen wire coat hangers. Then he rummaged through an old suitcase. "Mercury," he barked, "have you eaten all the pepper?"

"I certainly haven't eaten the pepper. Try looking in the bicycle basket, where you put it last month."

"Just where I thought it was," said Festus. He poured half a pound of pepper into the balloon. Then he blew up the balloon till it almost burst.

"Now we need some feathers," said Festus. "Have you got any feathers, Mercury?"

"I certainly haven't got feathers. Try asking the chickens."

Festus asked a bird name Prissy to collect feathers from the other hens. Prissy pursed her beak and went into the hen house while Festus untwisted the coat hangers and then shaped them into a frame around the balloon.

Prissy returned with a bag of feathers. "We want them back when you're done," she crowed sternly.

"Of course you'll get them back," said Festus. Then the old man and his cat pasted feathers onto the balloon. They made a comb and beak and pasted away until they had something that looked just like a chicken.

"Nice bird," said Mercury. "Why all the stuffing?"

"It's for the fox to sink his teeth in," laughed Festus. "When he sees her standing all by herself tonight, he'll pounce and BLAM! He'll be so scared by the noise and sneezing so hard from the pepper that he'll be cured of hens for good."

Prissy and the others applauded.

"Looks great," said Mercury when they stood the exploding hen in the yard. "But will it really do the trick? Why don't we make a few big bangs to be absolutely sure we scare that fox?"

"You may be right," Festus said. "Let's shoot off some fireworks."

They went back to the toolshed, and Festus turned over all the old paint cans. "Mercury, did you set off all the firecrackers?" he yelled.

"I certainly did not set off the firecrackers. Try looking in the hatbox, where you put them last July."

"Just where I thought they were," mumbled Festus, stuffing his pockets with fireworks.

They laid rockets and Roman candles all around the farm. Festus connected them with one long fuse and led it under the door, up the hall, and into the bedroom. He put a box of matches alongside the fuse.

"Okay," said Festus, "when that fox sinks his teeth into our exploding hen and we hear it go pop, I'll light the fuse and in no time the farmyard will be like judgment day. If that doesn't scare our fox, he must be pretty darned thick."

Mercury stared at the fuse for a moment. Then he said, "Foxes are pretty darned thick. I don't know that a few rockets will get it through his head that hens are off limits. We should make him think he's seen a ghost."

"A *ghost!*" growled the old man. But the more he thought about it, the more of a challenge it seemed. He looked all around the farmyard and had an idea. Then he led Mercury back to the toolshed.

"Mercury!" Festus roared, "Just last Monday I had a real long rope hanging right where that fiddle is. Did you lose that rope?"

"I certainly didn't lose that rope." Mercury groaned. "Try looking in the spare tire, where you put it last Tuesday."

"Just where I thought it was," mumbled Festus. He grabbed the rope and hunted up a white sheet and a pulley.

They stretched the rope from the roof to the big tree across the barn-yard and hung the pulley from the rope. "Mercury," said Festus, "how would you like to take a little ride?"

Mercury put on the sheet, climbed up the ladder, grabbed the pulley, and shot right over the yard and into the tree.

"That's perfect," said Festus. "Now tonight when I light the fuse, you run up to the attic and put on the sheet. Then when all the rockets are going off, you climb out the window and grab the pulley. When you're right over the fox, you howl like something from beyond the grave: THOU SHALT NOT STEAL CHICKENS! That should get the point across."

"It just might work," said Mercury. "Let's go in and have some supper." And they did.

It was a jittery evening. Festus packed all the hens into the kitchen and told them to take turns keeping watch at the window. If anybody saw the fox, Festus wanted to be awakened right away. Over and over Festus went out to check the booby-trapped hen, the fuse, the fireworks, and the pulley. Mercury kept practicing his line: THOU SHALT NOT STEAL CHICKENS!

Even after they'd turned in, the farmer and his cat kept going over the plan. They'd show Hiram, all right. That fox was never going to come within five miles of another hen! They were far too excited to go to sleep.

Mercury finally dropped off around midnight. But Festus lay there in the dark, staring at the ceiling. Then he thought he heard a noise. He peered out the window, and there was the fox, sniffing the ground around the hen house. The fox looked scared. He was pitifully thin, and one leg was lame.

That poor thing will have a heart attack if those fireworks go off, Festus thought. He decided not to light the fuse.

The fox crept up on the peppery hen. Suddenly he pounced — then stopped inches away. He sniffed at it cautiously, then dashed just beyond the fence. As Festus and the fox stared at each other, the old man could hardly stand the thought of Hiram shooting the poor creature. All was still and peaceful . . .

When BANG, the balloon exploded! Somebody started to cough and sneeze and wheeze. Mercury sprang out of bed shouting, "Light the fuse!" Not seeing Festus, the cat lit it himself. Through the rockets' red glare he dashed up to the attic, threw on the ghostly sheet, and wheeled across the rope, screeching "THOU SHALT NOT HUNT FOXES!."

Oops—he felt stupid for saying his line wrong, stupid until he looked down and saw not the fox but Hiram. The hound dog howled as Hiram stared at the spirit from on high, dropped his gun, and cried, "Help! I'll never hunt another fox again! Mercy!"

The dog ran away, Mercury vanished into the tree, the last Roman candle went off, and there was silence. Hiram trembled in the darkness. Then one last little firecracker whizzed by, and Hiram took off like a rocket.

Mercury jumped out of the tree and strolled into the kitchen. Festus sat there cackling with the hens. "Good job, Mercury. That fox won't be troubling us again."

"But Festus, that wasn't the fox, that was Hiram."

"Yes, but the fox was here, too, and he saw it all. After that peppery chicken blew up, he dashed into the kitchen and found a dozen hens staring at him. He was so scared he ran right back out again. And on his way out he grabbed the chocolate pudding we were saving for dessert tomorrow."

"He looked like he could use it," said Mercury. "And you wouldn't mind making another pudding, would you?"

Festus didn't mind in the least.

Mercury jumped out of the tree and strolled into the kitchen. Festus sat there cackling with the hens. "Good job, Mercury. That fox won't be troubling us again."

"But Festus, that wasn't the fox, that was Hiram."

"Yes, but the fox was here, too, and he saw it all. After that peppery chicken blew up, he dashed into the kitchen and found a dozen hens staring at him. He was so scared he ran right back out again. And on his way out he grabbed the chocolate pudding we were saving for dessert tomorrow."

"He looked like he could use it," said Mercury. "And you wouldn't mind making another pudding, would you?"

Festus didn't mind in the least.

E
NOR

Nordqvist, Sven,
The fox hunt

DATE DUE			
JUL 26 1989			
AUG 04 1989			
NOV 2 0 1989			
DEC 1 6 1989			
MAR 2 4 1990